To Simon
—J.C.

Published by
PEACHTREE PUBLISHING COMPANY INC.
1700 Chattahoochee Avenue
Atlanta, Georgia 30318-2112
www.peachtree-online.com

Text and illustrations © 2018 by Julie Colombet
First published in Great Britain in 2018 by Templar Publishing,
an imprint of Kings Road Publishing, part of the Bonnier Publishing Group
First United States version published in 2020 by Peachtree Publishing Company Inc.

The illustrations were rendered in pencil and colored digitally.

Printed in January 2020 in China
10 9 8 7 6 5 4 3 2 1
First Edition

ISBN: 978-1-68263-156-0

Library of Congress Cataloging-in-Publication Data

Names: Colombet, Julie, author, illustrator.
Title: The Society of Distinguished Lemmings / written and illustrated by Julie Colombet.
Description: Atlanta, Georgia : Peachtree Publishing Company Inc., 2020. | "First published in the United Kingdom
in 2018 by Templar Publishing"—Copyright page. | Summary: When the lemmings encounter a bear,
they are determined to help him be more "distinguished"—just like they are—but little do they realize
this bear could be exactly what they need to save them from themselves.
Identifiers: LCCN 2019019055 | ISBN 9781682631560
Subjects: | CYAC: Lemmings—Fiction. | Bears—Fiction. | Conformity—Fiction. | Individuality—Fiction. | Humorous stories.
Classification: LCC PZ7.1.C64493 So 2020 | DDC [E]—dc23 LC record available at *https://lccn.loc.gov/2019019055*

The Society of Distinguished Lemmings

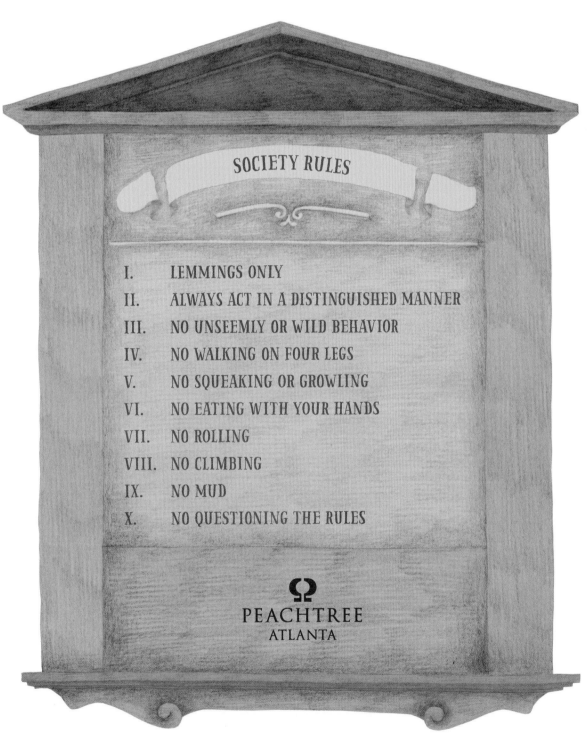

SOCIETY RULES

I.   LEMMINGS ONLY
II.   ALWAYS ACT IN A DISTINGUISHED MANNER
III.   NO UNSEEMLY OR WILD BEHAVIOR
IV.   NO WALKING ON FOUR LEGS
V.   NO SQUEAKING OR GROWLING
VI.   NO EATING WITH YOUR HANDS
VII.   NO ROLLING
VIII.   NO CLIMBING
IX.   NO MUD
X.   NO QUESTIONING THE RULES

PEACHTREE
ATLANTA

Julie Colombet

This is the Society of Distinguished Lemmings.

Deep in their underground burrow, the lemmings follow a strict
set of rules and are always very busy with social events.

They perform long
and serious plays.

They play the piano exceedingly well!

And every meal is a spectacle of fine dining.

BUUURP!

These leaves are the best I've ever eaten.

Nigel, that's your third glass!

My compliments to the chef!

In fact, there are very few areas in which the lemmings are not distinguished.

I've got it!

Good shot, Margot!

They never pick me for doubles . . .

SCORE

That said, the Society of Distinguished Lemmings
is not to everyone's taste.

This is Bertie, and he's had enough.
There is TOO MUCH noise in here.

So Bertie has decided to go outside.

Outside he finds there is a bear.

Bertie has never met a bear before.
He's heard they can be very fierce and scary
(not to mention awfully dim).

And the bear has never met a lemming before.
He's heard they can be talkative and annoying
(not to mention terrible show-offs).

Neither of them moves a muscle.

Then the bear leans down
and gives Bertie
a long, wet
lick.

The bear is clearly in
the mood to make friends!

Bertie shows the bear all his favorite things to do.
But the bear isn't interested in painting.

He isn't interested in chess, either. In fact, the bear
isn't interested in anything Bertie suggests.

Apparently the bear would
rather roll in the flowers

or climb a tree

or jump in muddy puddles.

And much to his surprise, Bertie finds
he'd rather do those things too.

It's not how things are done in the Society of Distinguished Lemmings
(in fact it breaks several rules), but it's nice to have a friend who's a little bit different.

Bertie and the bear are doing nothing in particular,
when there is a sudden rumbling under the ground.

Out of the burrow bursts a stream
of chattering lemmings.

They decide at once that the bear
is not at all distinguished.

But a bear can't join the Society!
What about the Society rules?
I want him to join the Society!
I suppose we could try to teach him . . .
Mind your step, Cyril!
This is unbearable.
Here we go . . .

If the bear is ever going to join the Society,
he will have a lot to learn.

First of all, he must learn to talk.

Proper posture is also very important.

And table manners are a must if he is
ever going to dine in fine society.

But the bear can't do anything right . . .

Before long, the lemmings decide enough is enough.
The bear will never be distinguished. And besides,
the lemmings have better things to do with their time.

It never occurs to them that the bear could be upset. But he is.
Because even though he is big and wild and not at all like a lemming,
he didn't want to disappoint Bertie.

But the lemmings have already moved on to other things.

With a lot of talk (but very little thought)
they decide to go on vacation—immediately!

Bertie and the bear haven't been invited, but they don't particularly mind.
On their own they can do whatever they want.

They walk to the top of the hill, and then Bertie pulls out his book and starts to read aloud.

That's when they make a terrible discovery.

"SOMETIMES LEMMINGS WILL DECIDE TO GO ON A VERY LONG JOURNEY,
CALLED A MIGRATION. IF LEMMINGS ENCOUNTER WATER AND TRY TO SWIM TOO FAR,
THEY WILL QUICKLY GROW TIRED AND MAY EVEN DROWN!"

I have a bad feeling about this.

A SHORT HISTORY OF LEMMINGS

Bertie and the bear start to worry.
The lemmings could be in all sorts of trouble without them!

They race across fields

and bound over bushes

and weave through trees.

But when they reach the shore, the lemmings have already left.

OH NO!

By now the lemmings have gone too far out into the ocean. At first they enjoy their swim.

Then they start to grow tired.

And before long, they are exhausted.

The water is deep, the lemmings are tired,
and it is a very long way back to shore.

Slowly, a strange shape appears over the horizon.
It grows bigger and bigger and begins to look oddly familiar.

It's a rescue mission! And it's arrived just in the nick of time.
The lemmings clamber aboard the bear, and their
brush with danger is quickly forgotten.

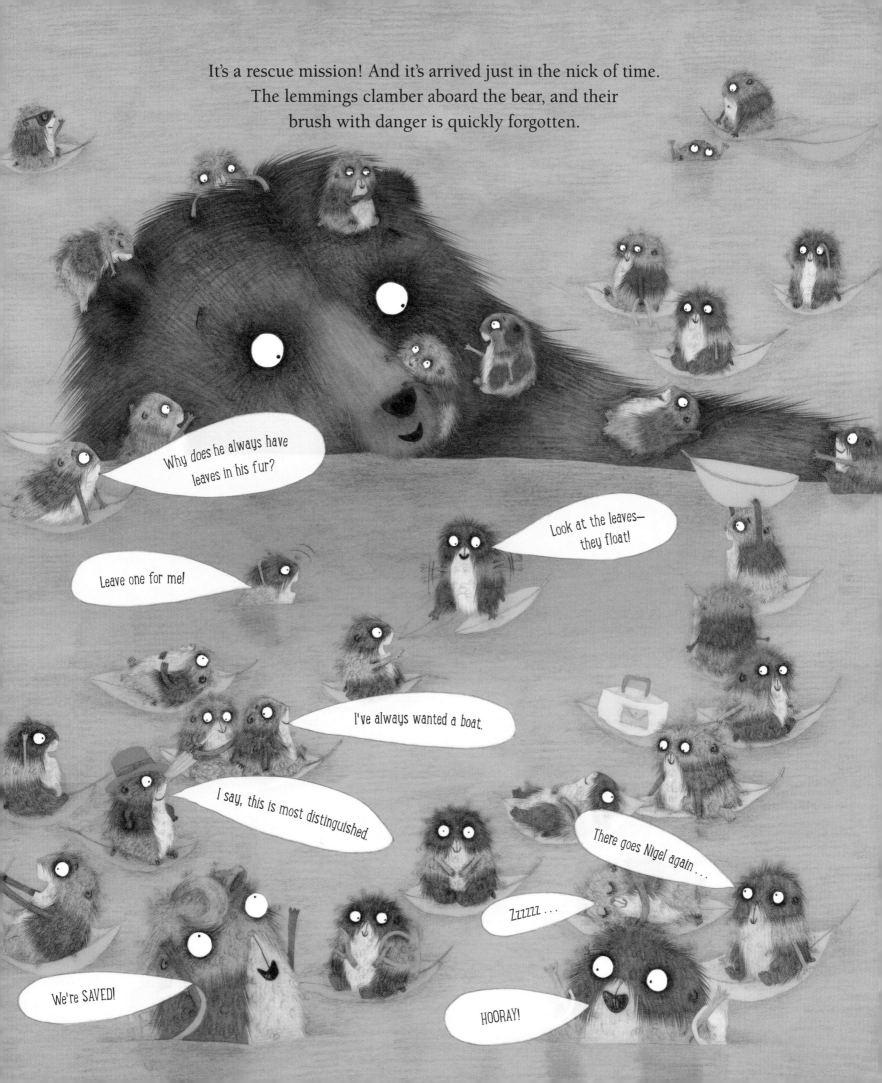

Back on the shore, Bertie calls the Society together for a hasty meeting. Everyone agrees that the bear must join the Society of Lemmings at once!

So with much ceremony (and many long speeches),
the lemmings formally welcome the bear to join them.

This is the Society of Distinguished Lemmings...
and Bears!

Their rules are a little bit different, but the lemmings
are still distinguished in all the ways that matter most.

Bear showed us a new game
called "mud rolling."

So what are the rules?

There are no rules!

The **Society** of **Distinguished Lemmings**

and Bears

BUUURP!

I've never been
to a picnic before . . .

It is distinguished—just
in a different way!

Alfresco dining
is delightful!

I think it's time for a new set
of rules, don't you?

And now they know that anyone can be distinguished,
in any way they choose.